Fancy NANCY

at the Museum

by

cover illus

interio

D1042417

HarperCollins *Children's Books*

Ooo-la-la!

I am overjoyed.

(That's a fancy word for very happy.)

Our class is going

to a museum.

I look extra fancy.

So does Ms Glass.

"I love your shirt,"

I tell her.

Ms Glass tells us,

"Today we will see masterpieces!

That's a fancy word

for great paintings."

The bus ride is very bumpy.

Bump! Bump! Bump!

Bree is my bus buddy.

"My tummy feels funny,"

she tells me.

Bump! Bump! Bump!

We stop for lunch.

Bree is not hungry.

But I am.

I eat my lunch.

I eat her lunch too.

I have two eggs,

a juice box,

carrot sticks,

an apple

and a big cookie.

"*Merci,*" I say.

(That's French for thank you.)

Now we are back on the bus.

Bump! Bump! Bump!

"We will be there soon,"

says Ms Glass.

I hope so.

My tummy feels funny now –
very funny.

Maybe two lunches was
one lunch too many.

"Ms Glass! Ms Glass!"

I cry.

"I am going to be sick."

"Stop the bus!"

Ms Glass cries.

The bus stops.

Ms Glass takes me

to the side of the road.

I am sick.

I drink some water.

I suck on a mint.

My tummy feels better.

But I am not overjoyed

any more.

I am all dirty.

"I wanted to look extra fancy today,"
I say sadly.

"I understand," Ms Glass says.

"And I have an idea."

We get to the museum.

"Come with me," says Ms Glass.

I come out.

Ms Glass's idea was spectacular.

(That's a fancy word for great.)

"Lucky you," says Bree.

"I wish I got to wear her shirt and hat."

"It is a French hat," I tell her.

"It is a beret."

A man from the museum

takes us to a gallery.

(That's a fancy museum word for room.)

I love all the paintings –
the masterpieces most of all.
We see paintings of trees and lakes.
They are called landscapes.

We see paintings of flowers
and bowls of fruit.
They are called still lifes.

The last painting is a picture of a lady.

"A painting of a person

is called a portrait,"

the man tells us.

"I like her hat and her fan and her beads,"

I tell the man.

"They are lavender.

Lavender is my favorite colour."

(That's a fancy word for light purple.)

The man smiles.

"You are a very observant girl."

Then Ms Glass tells us,

"Observant means noticing things.

Nancy is very observant, indeed."

On the bus trip back,

I do not feel sick.

I feel almost overjoyed.

That night,

I make a painting for Ms Glass

because she is so nice.

Merci from NANCY